Meet the People in Your Neighborhood

People in Your Neighborhood

Do you know the people in your neighborhood?

When Elmo walks with his daddy around his neighborhood, he sees lots of different people. His daddy tells him about all the places his neighbors go to work each day and about all the different jobs they do. Why don't you come along on a visit around the neighborhood?

Elmo lives near the Sesame Street firehouse. You might live near some **brave** firefighters, too. When there is a fire, a bell rings at the station. The firefighters slide down the firehouse pole to get dressed and go. They wear hard helmets and special **fireproof** jackets to protect them from the hot flames. To get to a fire quickly, they ride on a fire truck with a loud siren. Then they use long water hoses to put out the flames. Elmo really likes the color of this firefighter's helmet!

People in Your Neighborhood

Plumbers probably live in your neighborhood. Do you know what plumbers do? They fix sinks and toilets and bathtubs, so that everything is in working order when you need to use it.

Hopefully you won't need to call a plumber. But if you do, plumbers will work on pipes that are hidden inside your walls and under your floor. They will make sure the **pipes** are clean and clear, and they will fix leaky holes. They may need a special tool, like a **wrench**, to do their work. Look, Grover is ready to take a bath. Good thing the plumber already fixed all the pipes!

Stop

People in Your Neighborhood

You might live near a veterinarian. That's a long word—can you say it? Veterinarians are **doctors** for animals. Veterinarians care for small animals like cats, dogs, and birds. They also care for big animals like horses and cows.

Veterinarians—or vets, for short—use **medicine** and special instruments, just like people doctors. They usually see pets in their office, but sometimes they will go visit animals in homes or on farms. Vets help keep animals healthy and help them feel better if they are sick. It would be fun to be a veterinarian.

People in Your Neighborhood

Maybe musicians live in your neighborhood. Musicians are very talented! They play instruments like the **guitar**, 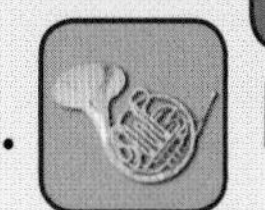 drums,  piano,  and French horn. It takes a lot of practicing to learn how to play an instrument.

After all that practice, musicians are ready to play in front of an **audience**. Elmo loves to go to **concerts** and be part of an audience. So does Zoe. They like to see musicians play on a stage or even in the park, in a band or orchestra. Elmo and Zoe also love to play musical instruments. Do you have a favorite instrument that you play or like to listen to?

Stop

Do you have any neighbors who have gardens? If you do, you can call them gardeners! Gardeners grow beautiful flowers, sweet fruits, fresh vegetables, and tasty **herbs** in a special space outside. Gardens need a lot of care, and growing a garden can take a long time.

First, **seeds** must be planted in the earth. Gardeners use special tools for planting. A shovel digs holes to bury the seeds in the soil. A rake mixes the soil around to keep it fresh. Next, the seeds must be watered. They also must get lots of sunshine. Water and sunshine help the seeds grow. After a while, the garden is filled with fresh food and colorful flowers, two things that Elmo loves. Don't you?

You might live near a librarian. Librarians love books, and so does Elmo! You can find librarians working in the **library**. Elmo has a library card, which he uses to **borrow** his favorite books to bring home. When he returns the books, librarians put them back on the shelf where they belong. If you have a library card, you can borrow books, just like Elmo. There are also movies, music, and other things at the library — so much to see and learn!

Librarians can help you find whatever you're looking for, and they can answer your questions. Librarians are some of the most helpful people Elmo knows. Thank you, librarians!

People in Your Neighborhood

Stop

Perhaps there is a chef in your neighborhood. Cookie Monster likes to spend as much time around chefs as he can. Can you guess why?

Chefs make yummy food to eat. They work in kitchens at restaurants or stores. Sometimes they wear puffy white hats and **aprons**. They bake some food in the oven and cook other food on top of the stove. They use tools such as spoons, measuring cups, spatulas, whisks, and a **blender**. 

Chefs make tasty foods with healthy ingredients—like this bread. Mmm! It smells great, and Cookie Monster says, "Cowabunga! Taste dee-licious!"

Stop

People in Your Neighborhood

Are there any zookeepers in your neighborhood? Zookeepers take care of animals at the zoo. Do you ever visit the zoo? What's your favorite animal?

Zoo animals are not pets. They are **wild** animals, such as lions and polar bears and elephants. Zookeepers must be very careful around such big, wild creatures when it's time to feed them and clean their **exhibits**.

The zoo is a good place to watch and learn about animals that you usually don't see in your neighborhood. Elmo loves visiting the zoo.

Stop

You might live near an architect. Architects don't build your hous
but they are the people who figure out *how* to build houses.

Architects must think long and hard about the plans for a new building. They measure very carefully to make shapes fit together, and they use **math** to make plans for each new building.

Architects draw their plans with special **rulers** and pencils, or with a computer. They make copies of the plans called blueprints—because they are printed on blue paper! Then architects work with a team of hard workers who actually do the building, carefully following the blueprints to make a shiny new home, school, hospital, or apartment. Elmo likes to draw shapes and buildings. Maybe someday he will be a good architect!

People in Your Neighborhood

Have you ever been on a boat? Sailors spend a lot of time on boats. They may live in your neighborhood, but they can also go anywhere the boat takes them. They can fish from the boat, travel to a **tropical** island, or just enjoy coasting on the water.

On a sailboat, sails use the wind to push the boat forward. Sailors make sure the sails are facing the right direction. Sailors keep **rope** to tie things down and life preservers to keep themselves safe. When Elmo pulls the **anchor** up from the bottom, he says, "Anchors aweigh!" Just like a real sailor!

People in Your Neighborho

Elmo loves to play sports. Do you? Elmo runs. He jumps. He stretches his **muscles**. People who play sports a lot are called athletes. 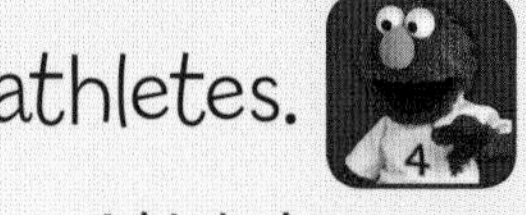 You might live near an athlete.

Athletes can play many different sports. They can play alone or on a team. They might kick the ball in a soccer match, swat the ball in a tennis match, or dribble the ball in a basketball game.

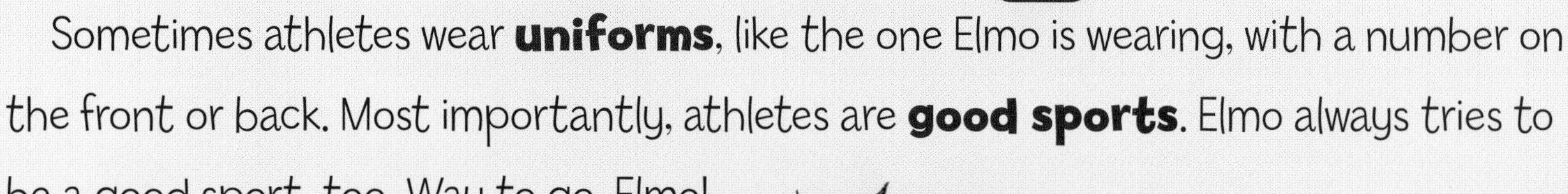

Sometimes athletes wear **uniforms**, like the one Elmo is wearing, with a number on the front or back. Most importantly, athletes are **good sports**. Elmo always tries to be a good sport, too. Way to go, Elmo!

Stop
2
4
3

People in Your Neighborhood

Do you know any teachers? If you go to school, you do! Many teachers work there, and some might live in your neighborhood. Teachers help you learn about lots of things at school. They help you read. They teach you about math. They help you learn about **science** and other things, too.

In the classroom, teachers tell stories and ask questions to solve problems. They use books, a board, and a **computer** to make learning fun. Best of all, the people in a classroom learn from one another.

Do you learn from your teachers? What have you learned so far about the people in your neighborhood?

People in Your Neighborhood

Have you ever been to a **museum**? Some museums have art. Some have bones from dinosaurs and ancient animals, or other old objects. Archaeologists are people who find those old objects. An archaeologist might live in your neighborhood.

Archaeologists search for clues about things that happened a long time ago. They dig in the ground for things like dishes, games, or bows and arrows, in order to study how people lived hundreds and even thousands of years ago. When archaeologists find something, they clean the object and give it to a museum **curator**. The curator puts it on display for people to see and learn from it.

Elmo and Cookie Monster love to visit the museum and see the things archaeologists have found. No eating cookies in the museum, Cookie Monster!

When Elmo looks at the sky above Sesame Street, he sees stars everywhere. He can't believe there are people whose job it is to study those stars! They're called astronomers, and one or two might live in your neighborhood.

Astronomers also study **planets**, the moon, and other objects in space. They use a **telescope** to zoom in and look at all those faraway things. They like to look at the sky when it's dark and the stars shine brightest. Elmo takes a turn looking into the telescope. There are too many stars to count, even for Elmo's friend, Count von Count!

There are so many different people who live in Elmo's neighborhood. They all have important and exciting jobs to do. Elmo hopes you get to know the people in your neighborhood, too!